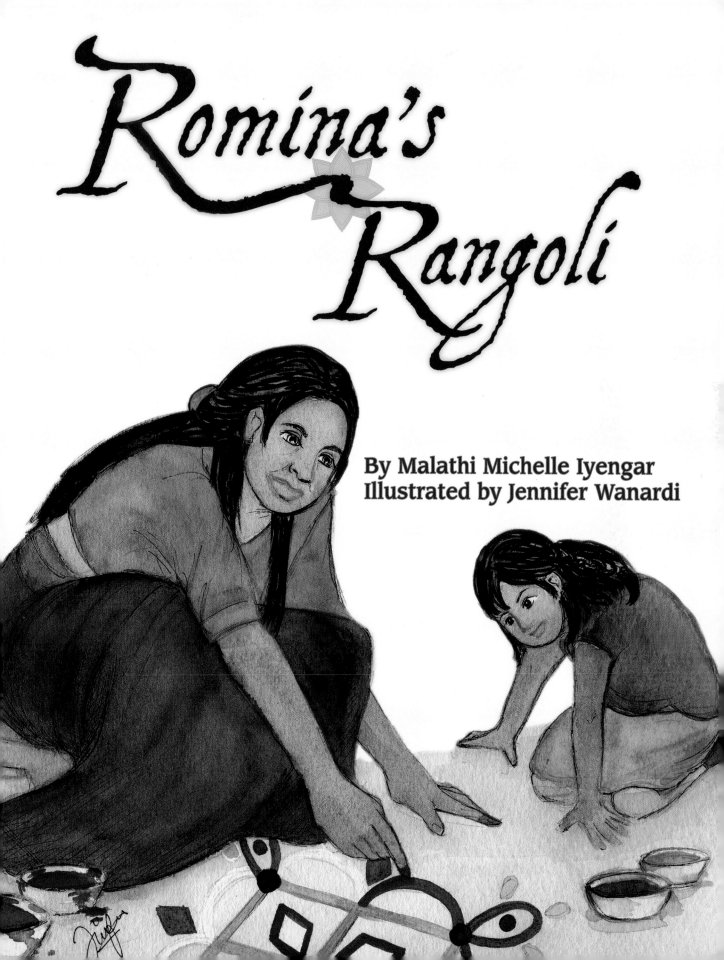

Romina's Rangoli

By Malathi Michelle Iyengar
Illustrated by Jennifer Wanardi

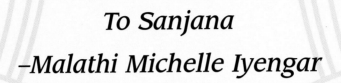

To Sanjana

–Malathi Michelle Iyengar

*To my mom, who always believes
in me and supports me in my life,
no matter what.*

–Jennifer Wanardi

Romina's Rangoli

By Malathi Michelle Iyengar
Illustrated by Jennifer Wanardi

"Boys and girls, this is Ireland," said Miss McMahan,
pointing to a tiny country on the world map.

Romina sat at her desk, twirling the end of her long,
black braid. Miss McMahan tapped the little country again.
"This is where my great-grandparents came from.
They were born and raised in Ireland,
and then they came to America."

Romina remembered how Miss McMahan had explained that people who left one country to settle in another were called *immigrants*. Romina's parents, like Miss McMahan's great-grandparents, were immigrants. Romina's father had come to the United States from India, and her mother was from Mexico.

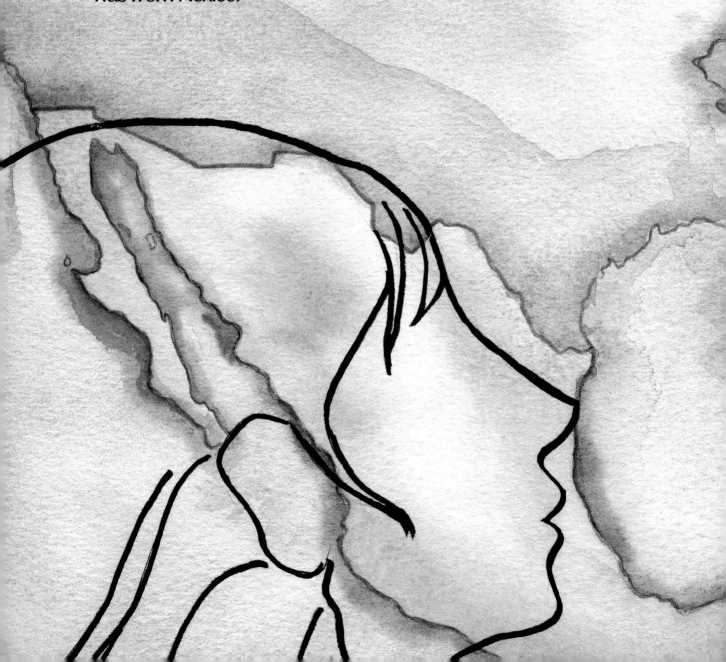

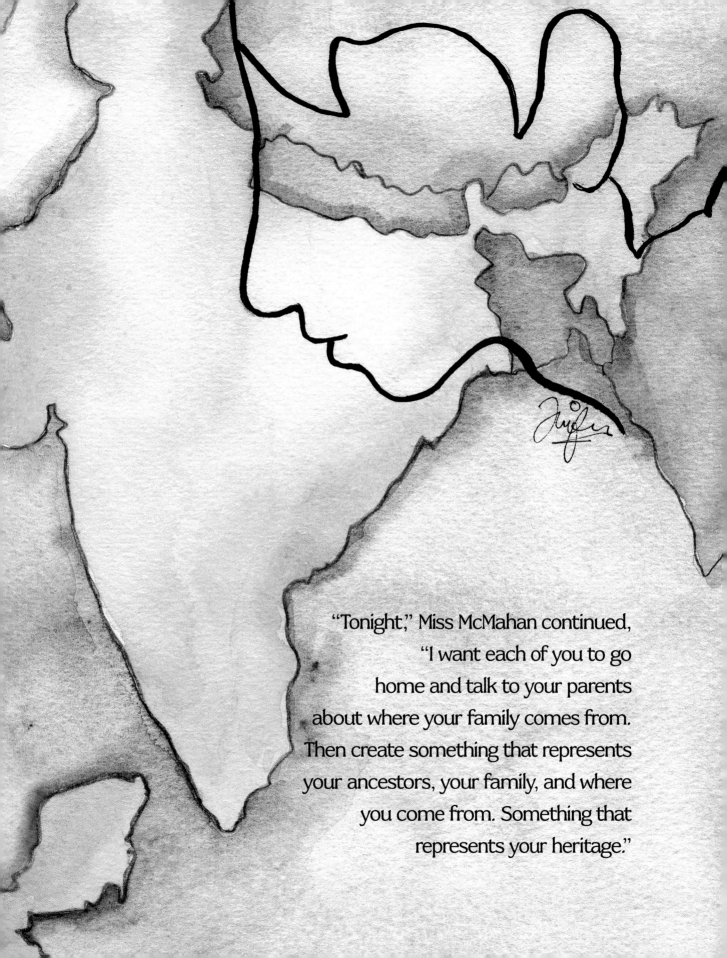

"Tonight," Miss McMahan continued, "I want each of you to go home and talk to your parents about where your family comes from. Then create something that represents your ancestors, your family, and where you come from. Something that represents your heritage."

Romina frowned. Make something to represent where her ancestors came from?

"You have all weekend to work on your projects. I know you'll all do a great job!" Romina looked down at her desk. "And," Miss McMahan continued, "since next week is our school Open House, your parents will be able to see your projects when they come to visit our classroom."

Just then the bell rang.

The children jumped up and headed for the door, talking and laughing.

Romina slowly picked up her backpack and walked over to Miss McMahan's desk. Miss McMahan smiled warmly. "Yes, Romina?" she asked. "What's on your mind?"

Romina wrinkled her brow. "Well ..." she murmured, "I ... I don't know what type of thing I should do for my project."

Miss McMahan laughed. "Is that all?" she asked. "Well, you don't have to come up with something right this minute! You have the whole weekend to think about it." Romina nodded weakly.

At home, Romina asked her sister, Leela, for help.
"Why don't you make some *rangoli* designs?"
Leela suggested. Romina closed her eyes and pictured the
intricate patterns and symmetrical designs she liked to draw
on the sidewalk with colored chalks, or make by arranging
different-colored flower petals on the front porch.
Then she opened her eyes and shook her head.
"No, Leela, I can't," she said. "Rangoli is from India.
And half of our family is from Mexico."

Leela shrugged. "Well, so what?" she asked.
"You can't do two projects."

But it's not that simple, thought Romina. Her parents would
both be coming to the school Open House next week.
How could she do a project that left one of them out?

Romina wandered into the kitchen. Her father was there, washing a bunch of cilantro. On the counter were some green chili peppers and her mother's large *molcajete*, or mortar.

"What are you doing, Appa?" asked Romina. "Are you making salsa?"

Appa laughed. "No, I'm making chutney. Spicey chutney to go with the *dosas* I'm about to make."

Romina watched as her father placed the chilies in the *molcajete* and began crushing them. "Chutney is a lot like salsa," she said, thinking aloud.

"That's right," said Appa, who loved to cook. "They use some of the same ingredients."

"Like cilantro and chili peppers," said Romina.

"Yes," Appa agreed, still crushing the chilies. "Actually, Indian foods and Mexican foods use a lot of the same ingredients. In India, we eat *dal.* In Mexico, people eat *lentejas.* *Dal* and *lentejas* are basically the same thing, lentils." Appa laughed again, picking up the cilantro. "Your mother and I may come from two different countries, but we do have at least one thing in common: we both love good food!"

Romina laughed, but then she frowned again. She couldn't take a bunch of cilantro to school. What would she do for her project?

In the living room, Romina's mother was sitting on the couch with a thick textbook and a pencil. Romina's mother was a graduate student.

"What's that?" asked Romina, peering at the textbook.

"This is a book of Nahuatl, *mija*," replied her mother. "It's a language from Mexico. I'm studying it in one of my classes."

"*Pero si en México se habla español!*" Romina exclaimed in surprise.

"*Sí, mija*," replied her mother. "People do speak Spanish in Mexico, but there are lots of other Mexican languages too."

"Lots of languages ..." Romina mused. "Just like in India!"

"True," her mother agreed. "There are dozens of languages in India."

*R*omina thought again about her family from Mexico and her family from India. *They have more in common than I thought*, she said to herself.

Romina got her chalks and went outside.
Sometimes drawing helped her think. On the sidewalk, she used a piece of white chalk to make five rows of five dots. Then she drew a blue border around the square of dots. Up and down, in and out and around, she drew graceful, curving lines that wove together around the dots to create a large *rangoli* pattern.

Suddenly she heard a deep voice call out,
"Aha, the artist is at work again! *La artista trabaja!*"

*R*omina looked up. There was her neighbor, Mr. Gonzales.

"How's life treating you, Romina?"

"Not so great, Mr. Gonzales," Romina replied glumly. She explained about her school project.

"But that's no problem for you, right *mija*? You can do your beautiful *rangoli*." Mr. Gonzales always stopped to admire Romina's *rangoli* designs whenever he walked by and saw her drawing on the sidewalk.

Romina groaned. "I can't do *rangoli* for my project, because *rangoli* is just from India, and my family is both Indian *and* Mexican. Besides, *rangoli* is floor art. It is made on the floor or on the ground, like how I'm drawing these *kolam* designs on the sidewalk. I can't take the sidewalk to school!"

"But *mija*," Mr. Gonzales answered, "your Mamá will understand if you want to make *rangoli* designs for your school project. Don't worry about it. We all know you're proud of being Mexican. Besides, those *rangoli* designs are great. I love all the symmetrical patterns. Some of them even remind me of the symmetrical pictures my mother used to make using *papel picado*."

Romina sighed. "I guess you're right," she mumbled. She looked down at the sidewalk, where she had woven together the lines of colored chalk to create her *rangoli* design. She remembered how her grandmother Ajji had taught her to draw this traditional *rangoli*, carefully demonstrating each line. This particular *rangoli* design, her Ajji had told her, was thousands of years old. People in India had been decorating the floors of their houses, entrances to temples, courtyards, and walkways with this design for centuries. "But I still don't know how to take my *rangoli* designs to school," thought Romina. "I can't pick up the ground, after all. I guess I'll have to draw my *rangoli* on a piece of paper, *una hoja de papel* ..."

*S*uddenly Romina jumped up. That was it! She knew what she could do for her project! "Mr. Gonzales!" she exclaimed. "Mr. Gonzales, can you show me how to make *papel picado*?"

"Me? Show you how to make *papel picado*?" Mr. Gonzales sounded surprised. "Well, I never was very good at that type of thing ... my mother was the real *papel picado* artist. But I guess I could show you the basics."

"Great!" Romina exclaimed.

"But I thought you were going to do *rangoli* for your school project," said Mr. Gonzales.

"I am," said Romina happily. "You'll see!"

On Monday, Romina arrived early for school. She couldn't wait to show off her project.

"Well, Romina," Miss McMahan smiled. "I see you came up with an idea for your project. Why don't you hang your picture on the wall? I'll give you some tape."

But, to her teacher's surprise, Romina began taping her picture, not to the wall, but to the floor in front of the classroom.

"Why are you putting your project on the floor?" asked Miss McMahan. "Is it a rug?"

Romina laughed. "No, it isn't a rug. It's a *rangoli.* A special kind of floor art. This design is hundreds of years old. My Ajji taught me how to make it when she visited us from India."

"Aha," said Miss McMahan. "So your project reflects your Indian heritage."

"Not *just* my Indian heritage," Romina corrected her teacher. "You see, in India this design would be made of different colored flower petals, or dyed rice-flour, or colored chalk. But mine is made of cut paper, *papel picado.*"

By this time, many of Romina's classmates had started to arrive. They gathered around the large, colorful *rangoli* made from *papel picado*. "Wow!" they exclaimed. "Cool!"

"So," said Miss McMahan to Romina, "your project is both Mexican and Indian. How interesting!"

"Yup," Romina agreed happily. "My project is both Indian and Mexican, combined. Just like me!"

Authors Notes:

Rangoli

An Ancient Folk Art from India

Rangoli, an ancient art form from the Indian subcontinent, is sometimes described as "floor art." Both children and adults create *rangoli* designs on their doorsteps, in front of their houses, at the entrances of temples, in the lobbies of buildings, on sidewalks, or simply on the bare ground. The different regions of India have their own distinctive styles and patterns of *rangoli*.

People use a variety of materials to create *rangoli*. One traditional practice is to make the designs using dry rice powder. Rice powder can also be mixed

with water to form a paste. Colored powders, pastes, and paints can also be produced using natural dyes, such as turmeric. Some people use flowers and flower petals to create bright (and fragrant) *rangoli* designs. People also use different types of dals, or dried legumes. Today, children and adults use not only the traditional materials, but also newer materials like synthetic paints and colored chalks to make *rangoli*.

Why do people make *rangoli* designs? Some folks like to make *rangoli* just because the designs are so beautiful. Other people attach religious or spiritual significance to the act of creating *rangoli*, or to the *rangoli* patterns themselves. In certain regions, specific *rangoli* patterns are associated with particular holidays,

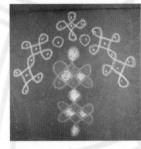

festivals, and ceremonies. Teachers also use *rangoli* designs to help students understand mathematical concepts such as rotational symmetry, exponential growth, and writing equations to extend patterns!

As you can see, the ancient Indian art form of *rangoli* is both beautiful and useful. Here's hoping this tradition will continue to grow and flourish, both in India and around the world!

Papel Picado
A traditional art form from Mexico

The art form now known as *papel picado* has its origins in pre-Columbian times, when Aztec cities were adorned with decorative paper sheets and banners in honor of special feasts and festivals. The material used for the Aztec banners was *amatl*, a type of paper made from wild fig tree and mulberry bark. Later, people began using tissue paper (sometimes called *papel de China*, or "Chinese paper") to make these lace-like paper hangings.

Throughout Mexico today – most famously in the state of Puebla – highly skilled papel picado artists use specialized chisels and blades to carve intricate patterns and designs in several layers of thin paper at once. Specific motifs, pictures, and colors are associated with particular occasions, such as the Day of the Dead,

Mexican Independence Day, Catholic holidays, and saints' days. Simpler *papel picado* pieces are commonly made by schoolchildren, who fold sheets of paper accordion-style and snip out symmetrical designs with scissors rather than using the sharp chisels and blades of adult craftspeople.

The art of papel picado as it exists today reflects a blend of materials, practices, and ideas from Europe, Asia, and the Americas. This lovely art form, with all of its variations and innovations, stands as a beautiful representation of the cultural and artistic hybrid of contemporary Mexico.

These *rangoli* and *papel picado* designs were made by the author, Malathi Iyengar. The photographs were taken by Kyle Baker.

Library of Congress Cataloging-in-Publication Data

Iyengar, Malathi.
  Romina's rangoli / by Malathi Michelle Iyengar ; illustrated by Jennifer Wanardi.
    p. cm.
  Summary: When her teacher asks each student to bring in something reflecting his or
her heritage to display at an open house, Romina struggles over how to represent both
her father's Indian culture and her mother's Mexican one.

  ISBN-13: 978-1-885008-32-9
  ISBN-10: 1-885008-32-5
  [1. Multiculturalism--Fiction. 2. Individuality--Fiction. 3. East Indian Americans--Fiction. 4.
Mexican Americans--Fiction. 5. Schools--Fiction.] I. Wanardi, Jennifer, ill. II. Title.

PZ7.19575 Rom 2007
[E]--dc22

                                        2006037892

Shen's Books
Fremont, California

Printed in China

Book Design and computer production: Patty Arnold, Menagerie Design and Publishing